the
BEAR and the
MOON

For my father —MB
To my Emmie bear —CC

The author would like to thank the Sacatar Foundation for the many
moonrises over the island of Bahia, Brazil.

Library of Congress Cataloging-in-Publication Data:
Names: Burgess, Matthew, author. | Chien, Cátia, illustrator.
Title: The bear and the moon / by Matthew Burgess ; illustrated by Cátia Chien.
Description: San Francisco : Chronicle Books, 2020. | Summary: "When the gift of a
balloon floats into Bear's life, the two companions embark on a journey of discovery
as small as a clearing in the forest . . . and as deep as the sky"— Provided by publisher.
Identifiers: LCCN 2019008767 | ISBN 9781452171913
Subjects: LCSH: Bears—Juvenile fiction. | Balloons—Juvenile fiction. | Friendship—
Juvenile fiction. | CYAC: Bears—Fiction. | Balloons—Fiction. | Friendship—Fiction.
Classification: LCC PZ7.1.B8743 Be 2020 | DDC 813.6 [E]—dc23
LC record available at https://lccn.loc.gov/2019008767

Manufactured in China.

Design by Mariam Quraishi.
Typeset in Directors Cut Pro.
The illustrations in this book were rendered in mixed media.

10 9 8 7 6 5 4 3 2 1

Chronicle Books LLC
680 Second Street
San Francisco, California 94107

Chronicle Books—we see things differently.
Become part of our community at www.chroniclekids.com.

the BEAR and the MOON

WORDS BY Matthew Burgess

PICTURES BY Cátia Chien

chronicle books · san francisco

Opening his eyes after a long snooze,
the bear saw a red dot in the blue sky.

The closer it floated,

the bigger
and rounder
and redder

the dot became . . .

. . . until it was no
longer a dot at all.

It was red as a berry
and round like the moon
with a long silver string
drifting brightly
in the breeze.

Curious, the bear went to investigate.

First, he tried to catch the
string between his teeth

but when it floated
out of reach, he climbed
onto a boulder and stood
on his two hind legs,
balancing.

Uh-oh.

The bear wobbled,
slipped, and tumbled
into a furry puddle.

Poor bear.

But then it drifted nearer . . .

and nearer . . .

There.

Suddenly, the bear felt lighter than air!

When he walked,
      it walked.

When he danced,
it danced.

And when dinnertime arrived,
he tied the silver string to a stone.

The bear enjoyed the quiet company
while he ate beside the creek,

and when evening became night,
it glowed softly in the moonlight.

The next morning, the bear
gave it a tour of his whereabouts.

Here is the tree
I can climb
to find honey.

Here is where
I curl into a ball
and roll down the hill.

And this is the spot
where I sit on the pot.

All the while, the floating red thing
smiled back at him like a friend.

It dipped and breezed and
bumped against the bear's cheek.

What a nice thing!
What a wonderful thing!
What a squishable, huggable thing!

Uh-oh.

The bear stared at the red tatter
dangling on the silver string.

He thought, *maybe I can fix it*?

He tried stretching it.

He tried throwing it back up into the sky.

He tried closing his eyes
and dancing with the string in his hand,
just as they had danced before.

But nothing brought it back.

The sky had sent him a gift,
a friend, a small red moon,
and now it was gone.

Bad bear,
he thought.

Bad, bad bear.

Night fell,
but the bear
skipped his dinner.

With a heavy heart, he listened to the water
rush over the rocks in the creek
and gazed up at the stars . . .

. . . when suddenly, the full moon
rose from behind two mountains.

It reached down to him
and gently stroked his fur.

Quietly, the moon was speaking to the bear,
and the bear understood.

Good bear.

Kind bear.

Don't worry, bear.

Blanketed in moonlight, the bear remembered
the small dot that grew and grew and grew into a
red round friend drifting brightly in the breeze.

It was gone now,
but as he dozed off to sleep,
he held the memory on a silver string.

And in his dreams, they danced again.